THE FAR SIDE
of Heaven

A Christmas Novella

D.L Gardner

ISBN-
9781393529279
Information may be obtained by
contacting
Dianne L Gardner at gardnersart.com

More works by the author as well as
video and audio are listed on the author's
website.
http://gardnersart.com

Cover design Les Solot Les
https://www.fiverr.com/
germancreative

*T*he Far Side of Heaven is dedicated to all of those who have had a hard time at Christmas and often feel they may be forgotten. I know I've had my share of sorrow during the holidays. May this little telling bring you a sense of hope, and some Light at the end of your tunnel.

D.L. Gardner

Charlene's Bane

"The fault, dear Brutus, is not in our stars,
But in ourselves."
-William Shakespeare, Julius Caesar

*I*f Charlene shut off her old pickup truck next to the ruins of her burned out house, she'd have to coast it down the hill and pop the clutch, and if that didn't get the engine going, she'd have to push the rubber-wheeled antique back up the hill by herself. That was a no-go on this icy incline, so she put the vehicle in park and with two hands, she hoisted the emergency brake lever.

"Darn thing still sticks," she mumbled, giving the brake a final yank.

Exhaust trundled into the air. The engine both sputtered and purred. She paused, her foot hovering over the clutch.

"Well? What are you going to do?" she asked the old Ford. "Run or stall?"

Charlene waited.

The engine spit a few times, then settled into a growl. She nodded and grabbed her gloves off the seat before planting her feet on the crunchy ice.

She pulled her wool scarf over her ears and tucked it in a knot under her coat close to her chin. Tugging her ski cap down over her head, she stepped away from the cab. She grabbed three milk crates out of the truck bed and headed toward the ruins that was once her home. The truck door swung open, the heater hadn't worked ever since her ex rewired the ignition so what did it matter?

Nothing of her former house remained. There was only a lone brick fireplace standing amid the rubble of a burned-out ranch house. Most of the debris had been cleared, the broken glass, the charred furniture, the wiring that had melted into the ground. Her parents had hired a crew to clean up the remnants with a backhoe after this summer's wildfire destroyed the forty-acre estate. She had no fire insurance. No one in Meritville did. Too many wildfires.

Because of that, property values had plummeted. Instead of trying to sell the forty acres, her parents signed a quit claim deed to the property for Charlene. They put a portion of their savings in the bank to help her pick up the pieces of her broken life and then her parents moved to Europe.

Perhaps someday Charlene would rebuild.

The only part of the ranch that hadn't been devastated by the fire was the root cellar which was a dug-out separate from the home. Today Charlene filled her crates with the last of the home-canned goods that had been stored there. Apples, peaches, canned plums. Even the green beans from last year's garden were still good. She'd need the extra food. With snow covering the mountain passes, their local grocery store was having difficulty keeping stocked. Tourism in her little town of Meritville would come to an abrupt standstill. It always did when winter set in unless the ski lodge twenty miles away brought visitors.

But why would they? Meritville had little to offer folks from the big city.

Charlene's shop had weathered the lack of tourism in the past, but that was before the fire took so many homes. The population had declined drastically. Like her parents had, Meritville folks moved elsewhere. It was a wonder that the little community hadn't become a ghost town.

Christmas was going to be cheerless this year.

The Shop

"I've learned a long time ago not to depend on the Meritville Mercantile to feed us" - Charlene

Charlene noticed Jill Newberry standing outside the Cozy Home Gift shop that also served as a library and coffee shop. When Charlene drove up, her friend pulled her hands out of her downy coat and waved, steamy breath leaking from under her turned up collar. The store wouldn't open for an hour so to see Jill with her teeth chattering and stomping her boots on the brittle sidewalk surprised Charlene.

"I'll be right there. I've got to park this battle-axe on the hill. Meet me around the corner and you can help me carry a crate." Charlene stopped in the street and shouted out the half-opened window.

"Got ya!" Jill agreed.

The truck skidded when Charlene turned right on Oarlock Street, wheels spinning. She gunned the vehicle up the hill, made a U-turn by the alley and pulled up alongside the curb. Turning her wheels inward and with a strong

11

hoist on the emergency brake handle, she shut off the engine. She quickly jumped out and retrieved two bricks from the truck bed and tossed them on the ground. With her boot, she kicked them in front of her tires. Jill trudged up the hill to meet her.

"What did you get this time?" Jill asked as Charlene pulled the crates out of the truck.

"Food."

"Food? You worry too much," Jill said.

"And you don't worry enough, Jill. I've learned a long time ago not to depend on the Meritville Mercantile to feed us."

"It's not like Lewisville is eons away. It only takes an hour to get there."

Charlene looked at her friend's brilliant blue eyes peeking out from under the woolen ski hat.

"You jest," Charlene said.

"We could take my car," Jill added meekly after a quick examination of Charlene's truck.

"Thanks for recognizing this gas guzzling jalopy isn't road-worthy!" She carried the weight of two filled crates down the hill with Jill carrying the other. "There's a big storm-front coming from Alaska this week. Should be hitting Washington tomorrow."

"Christmas Eve is Thursday," Jill reminded her.

"Yes, ma'am."

"Shoot. That means we probably won't have power on Christmas." Jill pouted.

Charlene set her boxes on the sidewalk and slipped the key to her shop into the keyhole. Icicles hung from the eaves above her and frost covered the corners of the door's window.

"What Christmas? Or should I say what's Christmas?"

"You're such a humbug," Jill complained as the two pushed their way into the store with arms loaded. "My nephews from the coast are supposed to be here Wednesday."

"Your nephews will be snowed in."

"That's OK. They like snowboarding."

"How are they getting here?"

"The train. They're arriving tomorrow night and we're supposed to go shopping together in Lewisville. *Brr.* Turn the heat on!" Jill set the box of food on one of the tables in the dining area.

The Cozy Home Gift Shop had two tables and a kitchen, but it wasn't really a restaurant of sorts. It was a library first and foremost because Charlene's father, who had started the business and then signed it over to her when they left, had been an avid reader and book collector. It had been his idea to open the library and offer scholastic opportunity to the rural residents of Meritville. Only after Charlene's divorce did he give the store over to her and she added to

13

the inventory by buying books wholesale and offering them as merchandise. She promoted local authors by writing reviews in a column in the local newspaper and letting them have book signings.

With tourism a primary resource for Meritville's economy, Charlene purchased customized gift items to put in the shop and soon she had soaps and crafts made locally, and tourist relics to remind travelers that there indeed existed a little town called Meritville. Since she spent all day in the store, she purchased an espresso machine and offered coffee, tea, and homemade breads and cookies for customers who wanted to linger. Mrs. Jameston did the baking. Hence, the dining area.

Charlene deactivated the security alarm, turned on the heat and picked up her crates again. "We're taking these upstairs."

Jill grunted and followed her up the creaking rungs at the back of the store. "This is hard," she complained. "You really do need to get these stairs fixed. What if I tripped and broke my hip?"

"You're not old enough to break your hip. C'mon Jill, be a big girl."

At the top of the stairs, Charlene goaded the door open and stepped into the tiny flat she had made a home out of. A foam cushion on the floor served as a bed. She set her crate on an old folding table and pushed the microwave up against the wall. Her clothes were folded neatly in boxes in the far corner of the room.

Jill set her crate down and looked around.

"I thought you were going to get some furniture in here."

"Didn't happen. Besides, Sheriff Bandon says I have to move out in the spring. He said it's illegal for me to take up residence here." She tossed a kitchen towel that had been wadded on the table into her pile of laundry.

"He's not going to evict you what with the fires and all is he?"

"Not now. But as soon as the weather turns, he will."

"Over my dead body!" Jill tossed her blond hair behind her shoulder and put her hands on her hips. Charlene chuckled at her. Always there to stand up for her friend.

"What are you going to do? Fight the sheriff?" Charlene asked.

"No. I guess not. You can move in with me. You might as well. You shower there, you do laundry there. Why not?" Jill inspected the jars in the crate.

"It wouldn't work. I'm too independent to move in with you, Jill. You know that."

"You're stubborn is what you are."

"Is that what it is?" Charlene looked her friend in the eye. "You have too many house guests. You don't want that room occupied. What about your nephews? And your niece? She'll be staying with you in the summer when she works at the lodge. It wouldn't be fair to your family. Besides, what happens in the spring is the furthest thing from my mind. I'm worried about what happens tomorrow if the power goes out."

"I guess." Jill pulled a jar of apples out of the crate and held it up to the light. "Too bad that beautiful orchard went up in flames."

"I don't want to talk about it, Jill." Charlene moved the jars off the table. There had to be some place they wouldn't be in the way.

"Sorry," Jill said.

"I grew up on that ranch. A lot of wonderful childhood memories disintegrated...," she inhaled and flushed the image of that blazing night out of her mind. "I just don't want to talk about it."

"I'll let it rest," Jill whispered. "And start the coffee."

The jingle of the doorbell alerted Charlene before Jill got to the bottom of the stairs.

"I brought in the newspapers." Mr. Atwater's voice came through crisp and clear. He was a regular customer who visited every morning to read his daily paper and drink coffee. *He's early*, Charlene thought, but in this weather, any customer was a good customer.

Charlene transferred the crates to a corner of the room and hurried down the stairs.

"Good morning, Mr. Atwater!" she greeted and tapped the thermostat up a notch. She knelt next to the potbelly stove in the corner and made a fire, adjusted the vent, and shut the door. She would burn just enough kindling to take the chill away, then let the furnace warm the shop for the rest of the day. For such a small space, heating the room took forever.

"Mmm," the tall, balding man mumbled. He sat down in his favorite spot and thumbed through one of the newspapers before pushing a dollar bill to the end of the table as payment. Charlene snatched it up immediately.

"Some new books came in last week. I thought you might like to look over some of the titles. They might interest you." Walking to her cash register, an antique as old as her truck, Charlene pressed the series of keys to open it. The till rang, a drawer popped out, and she carefully counted cash from her pocket to slip inside for the day's sales. She'd been robbing her savings account for a while to keep the business going. If everything worked out as planned, she'd have enough for rent and utilities until the tourists returned in the summer months.

"You know I don't read books," Mr. Atwater said as he opened the *Lewisville Daily* and buried his face in the financial section.

"Christmas will be here in three days. Surely you have a family member who reads," Charlene offered.

"Nope."

Charlene frowned at the man. His appearance was as ordinary as his monotone voice. Pale skin, pale eyes, pale expression on his elongated face.

Jill poured him a cup of coffee.

Charlene both appreciated Mr. Atwater and despised him at the same time. He'd been taking advantage of her cozy store for over a year now, coming in every day and buying a paper and a 50-cent cup of coffee, and never once had he bought anything from her store. She'd name him Scrooge if she thought he wouldn't get angry. Still, that dollar-fifty was cash she could count on every morning. *It might even pay the day's power bill if it weren't this cold outside.*

"I'm leaving," Jill announced. "As much as I love helping you, the restaurant hasn't laid me off yet and I need to make some money before they do."

"I'll be fine," Charlene assured her.

"The diner plans on shutting down on Christmas. What are you going to do on that special day?"

Charlene shook her head. She didn't know what to expect with the storm, and she might have to tend to something in the shop. If

18

the pipes froze, she would be in a real mess.

"I'll be open, Jill. I live here. Come on over and maybe we'll...I don't know, play cards or something."

"I'll have my nephews. The Scouts will be caroling again this year on Christmas Eve. My nephews will be going with them."

"They're welcome to hang out here on Christmas day, too, if you want," Charlene offered.

"All right. We'll talk later. I'll bring you some lunch this afternoon."

Jill poured herself a thermos of coffee, wrapped her coat tighter around her neck, pulled her scarf over her nose and nodded a goodbye.

Charlene tended to the shelves, dusting, rearranging the little bit of inventory she had. Four months had gone by since she was able to restock, but what did it matter? Tourists weren't coming in. No one in town would buy Meritville Mercantile-shaped piggy banks with the words *Welcome to Meritville* on them, not unless they were really hard up for Christmas presents. Most everyone in town had one of everything Charlene sold. Folks could only buy so much of the same thing. Still, there was a camaraderie here and people did what they could to support the few local businesses in town.

Except for people like Mr. Atwater who

lived on a huge ranch a few miles down the road. He drove a brand new Lexus but wouldn't take the blessed thing out of the garage on rainy days. Instead he drove his Lincoln in wet weather. He complained about the price of coffee and never left a tip, and yet spent his morning at Charlene's table reading the stock exchange. All Charlene could do was be cordial. Perhaps he'd soften in time. Maybe soon. After all it *was* Christmas.

Like that will happen, she thought to herself while giving him an evil eye. *There's been plenty of time for him to be congenial.*

Jill had decorated the shop for Christmas. She strung white lights around the storefront window and set up an artificial tree. Books, coffee mugs, and trinkets nested in fluffy cotton sprinkled with glitter. Not a huge display, but enough to show people that the Cozy Home acknowledged the season. Charlene hadn't had time, nor the inspiration to add to the decorations. Christmas had meant something before her home burned to the ground. Family, good cooking, even church. Now...well, now there just wasn't a reason.

She stooped and unlocked the glass case where more expensive antiques were housed. It was mostly tools from some of the older ranches in the area: snippers for shoeing horses, a butter churn, old wolf traps. Charlene seemed to just magically acquire the kind of things no one used anymore but were too intriguing for her to toss. After all, they might sell…. someday.

While dusting the shelf, Charlene sighed, thinking of the ash and embers she had to clean away at the ranch. Life seemed to be an endless motion of picking up broken shards and clearing away the dust. She stopped dusting when the bell to the door jingled. Mr. Atwater glanced up from his paper and Charlene stood to greet the two young men who walked in.

"Good morning!" Charlene said.

"Hello," one of the men said. They were obviously from the ski resort. They smelled like fresh snow and had that look about them. The cutting edge jackets that no one in Meritville could ever afford, the thick insulated gloves, the scarves, the healthy tan smiles. Charlene peeked out the window at their Jeep, snow in a pile on its roof.

"How might I help you two?" Charlene asked. "This is the Cozy Home Gift shop, so make yourselves at home. We've got coffee, books, gifts."

"Coffee would hit the spot for me," the man in red said and slugged his partner on the arm. "What do you say, Dallas? Let's park for a bit."

"I'm intrigued by the books," Dallas said.

She caught a glance from his hazel eyes

when he wandered past her to the bookshelves along the wall.

"This is amazing!" he exclaimed. "A gift shop and bookstore all in one? With coffee? It's really down home country, isn't it?"

"Down home, right. Where are you fellas from?" Charlene asked.

"L.A.," they chorused. Dallas browsed the library while the man in red studied the overhead menu. Seeing he might want something, Charlene set her dust cloth down and joined him.

"Coffee. Black," the man ordered. "Dallas, you want something?"

"Yes, Lew!" Dallas answered and strolled over to them. "Coffee. And maybe one of those peanut butter cookies you've got on display. Did you make those?"

She couldn't stop staring at him and almost didn't hear his question. Had it been that long since she noticed a good looking man?

"Those are made by a resident here in Meritville," Charlene answered as she poured them both a cup and handed Dallas his cookie. He smiled a delicious smile and slipped her a twenty-dollar bill. She groaned. Change wasn't easy to come by since the nearest bank was an hour away. Maybe she could borrow some change from Jill if she ran out of coin later in the day.

"Amazing till you have," Dallas said. "It's an antique?"

"It was my dad's, and his parents' before that."

"Have you lived here all your life?" Dallas asked.

"For the most part. Enjoy." Charlene might have sounded curt, but that was enough talking about her life. The scars were too fresh, and she shied away from men in general. The two took their coffee and sat at the table across from Mr. Atwater. Charlene left them and hid behind her dusting.

It didn't take long for the men to move from their table to Mr. Atwater's. Charlene glanced up, curious as to why. Mr. Atwater wasn't known for his friendliness.

"I can see by the section of newspaper you're reading, you're an investor. You play the stock market?" Charlene heard one of the men ask.

"I don't play, I invest," was Mr. Atwater's reply.

"Would you like to hear about a tangible investment? Something you can sink your teeth into?"

Charlene squinted at them through the glass case. What was that about? They spoke quietly and she couldn't hear all of their conversation. She stood, watching from behind the till, fidgeting with the dust rag. Was this something she was going to have to disrupt?

Dallas had pulled out a package from under his jacket, set the parcel on the table, and when he opened it, out sprang a full sized jacket.

"You won't believe the response we're getting with these," Dallas said. "You're an investor. Let me tell you, this is the hottest thing to ever hit the slopes. And they're compact. Survival wear." His eyes were wide with excitement.

Mr. Atwater held his paper folded in front of him and glared at them, saying nothing. But Charlene knew the man's temper and thought she had better interrupt whatever they were doing.

"You've heard of crowdfunding," Lew leaned over the table. Poor Mr. Atwater couldn't get away if he wanted to.

"Child's play," Mr. Atwater grumbled. "I don't ski."

"Just look at the material."

"Excuse me," Charlene stood over them. "What's going on?"

"We're just showing this gentleman our project,"

The interruption gave Mr. Atwater the break he obviously was waiting for. He stood, folded his newspaper, and gave Charlene a look that sent blood rushing to her forehead.

"I come here for peace and quiet, not for solicitors hounding me every few minutes!" With that the man stormed out the door.

"You were soliciting in my store?" She accused, jerking both ends of the dust cloth. Dust puffed into the air

"We saw he was an investor. He mentioned he liked our..."

"You don't sell your product in someone else's store. You should know that." Her cheeks flushed.

"We didn't mean any harm, really. We were just sharing our project with him. Anyone who reads the financial section of the news certainly has an interest in investment. We thought we'd..."

"Well, you can take your project back to the slopes with you."

Great, Charlene thought. *Three days before Christmas and I lost the only steady customer I ever had. And the only two tourists in town.* She threw the rag on the glass counter, breathing heavily. *Why do these kinds of things always happen to me?*

"We're dreadfully sorry, ma'am. We didn't mean to chase him away," Dallas said.

"You should know better than to solicit in someone else's business."

"We weren't really soliciting; we were
25

talking about our crowdfunding campaign. We weren't really selling anything," Lew claimed. "A casual conversation is all. We certainly didn't mean to upset him."

Dallas bowed his head.

"Yeah, no, she's right, Lew. How can we make up for it?" he asked Charlene.

"Well you can't, really. He's gone. He probably won't be back until tomorrow morning. If at all. I'm sure he won't accept an apology. He's not the kind of person that forgives and forgets. And if you aren't going to purchase anything else, then you should probably leave too."

Lew nodded and started for the door with their package tucked under his arm, but Dallas tugged at his sleeve.

"We'll buy something from the shop. How about it, Lew?" Without waiting for his friend's response, Dallas strolled over to the books.

"I'll wait in the car." Lew walked out of the store, the bell ringing a goodbye as he shut the door.

Charlene glanced at Dallas. He had his back to her and pulled off his ski cap, his thick dark hair fluffed around his ears as he skimmed the many books on the shelves. She probably shouldn't have suggested they buy something. She'd be better off if he just left. Her stomach was upset enough as it was, and having the man wandering around in her shop after what transpired was awkward.

She ignored him, sat in the chair behind her till and pulled her phone from her apron. She'd call Jill, but Jill was working and what would she say to her, anyway? "Help, there's a strange man in my shop?" Her hands shook.

Why? Why was she trembling? Sleepless nights on the floor? An ex she had to worry about coming around to haunt her? Financial ruin? What in her life could possibly be the cause of all this stress?

A tear dropped onto her apron and she pulled a tissue from under the counter. Charlene covered her face with her hands and moved her chair so that her back was to the library. Tears leaked out of her eyes and she wiped them and blew her nose. She needed to stop crying. This was no way to run a business. She wiped her cheeks and took a deep breath. She glanced over her shoulder. There was Dallas standing at the counter staring at her.

He had in front of him a pile of books and a couple of Meritville miniature piggy banks.

She blew her nose again, tossed the tissue in the trash, and stood. She drew a dollop of sanitizer from the dispenser and wiped her hands.

He didn't say a word while she rang up the merchandise. She made a note of the books he chose. A mystery written by one of Meritville's residents, Trudy Hammond, signed; a book on local wildlife with pictures, a brief history of Meritville that the historical society put out.

She found a paper sack recycled from the Mercantile, and packed his purchases, wrapping the banks in newspaper so they wouldn't scratch, and took his money. When she did look into his eyes, his gaze was deliberate, soul-searching.

Good heavens, what does he want? she thought.

"You make delicious coffee," he said softly.

"Jill made it."

"I'm terribly sorry. If there's anything else I can do."

"No. You're fine."

Just go away, she thought. *Go back to your ski slopes and have a good time with your friend, your project, and your life.*

The Flat

*"For he would be thinking of love
Till the stars had run away
And the shadows eaten the moon."
-W.B. Yeats, Selected Poems and Four Plays*

I once made my sister cry," Dallas said as he tossed his paper sack of merchandise into the back of the Jeep, thumping his head on the door frame as he fell onto the seat. He rubbed the knot on his head and looked at Lew. Lew's thumbs dashed over the keyboard of his cellphone. The engine ran, the heater blew hot air.

"Lew?"

"Just a minute," Lew responded.

"That shop owner left me puzzled. I didn't think we did anything to warrant tears. Did you?"

"Tears? She's crying?"

"Yes."

"Women get like that around the holidays. Weepy," Lew said, still texting. Snowflakes the size of a child's fists fell silently on the windshield. Lew switched on one sweep of the wiper and then turned it off.

29

Dallas' heart ached and he glanced at the shop window. The image of the woman weeping behind her till did not sit well with him. He would never intentionally cause someone that much pain.

"I wonder if there's something else wrong. You know, like money. This place seems economically challenged. Or empty. Like a ghost town. It's depressing," Dallas pondered.

"Mmm," Lew pushed send and waited.

"We should get back to the lodge. It's starting to snow," Dallas urged.

"We have a flat," Lew stated.

"What?"

"We have a flat tire."

"Well, let's get it fixed," Dallas unbuckled his seat belt.

"Where?" Lew held up the search he did on his phone. "There are no tire repair shops in Meritville. Closest one is in Lewisville an hour away." He blinked when he looked up at the snow. "Maybe two hours away."

"I told you we should have fixed the spare when we had the chance," Dallas complained. "Surely there's a gas station here."

"Yes. It's that way." Lew pointed into the blizzard that now blanketed them.

"God!" Dallas whispered.

"God may hear you, but I don't think He fixes flats."

Dallas threw open the door and stepped outside. Already the snow had collected in a sleek cushion at his feet and clung to his coat within seconds. He stomped to the back of the vehicle and pulled out the jack. Lew grabbed the lug wrench and the two of them took turns loosening lug nuts and removing the tire.

No headlights busied the town. Not a single soul had even stepped outside much less started a vehicle. All of Meritville seemed to have fallen asleep. Christmas lights sparkled over the dim city, in shop windows and on trees and flower containers along the street. Though it was still early in the day, the clouds shut out sunlight. Dallas felt as if he had stepped into some kind of seasonal TV advertisement.

"It's quite moving, actually," he said.

"What? The tire?"

"The town. You don't see places like this in southern California. Snow at the ski lodge, yes, but that's a totally different atmosphere. Listen to how quiet it is. I feel I'm in a whisper."

Lew shook his head.

"Your poetic side has always baffled me. It's frigging winter, we've got a flat tire and we're twenty miles from a hot shower and a warm bed. And you're creating holiday jingles."

"It's Christmas, Lew. I can't help feeling melancholy at Christmas."

"It's winter!"

Dallas shrugged and laughed.

"We're not going to freeze to death, man. We've got the warmest jackets in the country."

"We might not freeze to death, but we might have to sleep in the Jeep if we don't get a tire on this baby and get up the mountain." Lew tossed the jack and lug wrench into the back of the Jeep and slapped the door shut.

"You think that lady in the shop would give us a ride?"

"You dare ask?" Lew huffed a laugh as he rolled the tire into the street.

Dallas looked into the shop window again. It might be daring to ask her a favor, but he'd like to talk to her. Comfort her or something.

"I'd rather take my chances with her than walk in a blizzard. The worse she can do is say no."

"Or give you the dragon eye." Lew rested the tire against the Jeep and threw up his arms and. "It's your move."

Dallas returned to the Cozy Home Gift Shop, stomped his boots on the welcome rug, and shut the door. A fire cackled in the potbelly stove where the shop-keeper sat in a chair, quietly reading a book. He took a few steps toward her, enjoying the warmth of the stove and the sweet smell of cedar wood burning.

She looked up.

"I thought you left."

"I did. I got as far as the car. We have a flat tire."

Charlene stared at him, the book opened on her lap, her brown eyes blank.

"We were wondering if...I mean, is there someplace we could get it fixed? It's snowing out there," Dallas said.

The woman glanced out the window, a ray of light filtered gently across her face. She had rosy cheeks, and a few freckles that bridged her nose. The red highlights in her chestnut hair shimmered like copper threads.

"You're afraid of snow? I thought you were a skier," she asked.

He should have laughed. She probably meant it as a joke, but his face heated up and he was suddenly uncomfortable.

"I'm sorry to bother you." He headed for the door. Foolish of him to even suggest a favor after how they'd treated her. Of course, he and Lew could roll a tire down the road to a gas station. Not the most difficult task. Not much harder than cross-country skiing. Which he also had done.

"Wait," Charlene said. She stood before he got to the exit. "I have a truck. You have to coast it down the hill to get it started and you can't turn it off, but it will get you to where you're going." She tossed him the keys. Put it back where you found it, facing downhill."

33

Dallas gawked at her.

"You're going to lend us your truck? Just like that?"

"It's a piece of junk really. Sometimes I think I'd be better off without it. Anyone willing to steal the thing is welcome to it." She laughed. "But you might have a hard time getting out of town. It doesn't take kindly to highways. And if you break down in the snow, well, that's it."

Dallas stood motionless with the keys in the palm of his hand, not sure if he should accept the offer.

"Look. This is what people in the country do for each other. Besides," her voice softened, and her shoulders relaxed. "It's Christmas."

Dallas swallowed, a bit overwhelmed. No one in L.A. would toss their keys to a stranger, not for their life.

"I should probably know your name, in case someone recognizes your truck, I mean. They'd wonder what we're doing with it."

"Oh, they'll know my truck all right. I don't think there's a man in Meritville that hasn't tinkered with it in one way or another. My name is Charlene Donne. And you're Dallas."

"Yes, Charlene. As in the city in Texas. Although I've never been there."

"It's an Irish name. I had an uncle named Dallas. It means Valley of Water. You've got an Irish look about you. It's the nose, I think. Last name?"

"O'Neill."

"Yep." Charlene grinned. "Listen, the truck does good in the snow, but if you want to make it back up the hill where you started, you'd better hurry. They say it isn't going to stop snowing until after Christmas."

"Where is it?" Dallas asked.

"To your right, around the corner on Oarlock Street at the top of the block. The old truck looks black but it's really blue. '57 Ford. The running boards are rusted, and the emergency brake is a devil to release. There are bricks in front of the tires. Throw them in the back of the truck and don't forget to put them back after you park."

"Thank you, Charlene."

She nodded.

Dallas hurried out the door tossing the keys in his hands. He jiggled them in front of Lew.

"Wait here, I'll come get you."

It was a good thing Dallas had a little experience with old trucks. Popping the clutch wasn't that hard to do, though the vehicle did skid a little on the ice as he came to the intersection.

"I can't turn it off," he called to Lew.

His friend tossed the tire in back and jumped in the passenger seat.

"Which way?" Dallas asked while Lew fidgeted with his GPS.

"Straight down the road."

"What road?"

Indeed, the snow had fallen so heavily that any semblance of a road had disappeared. If there hadn't been streetlights and Christmas lights dangling over them, Dallas would not have been able to navigate. Fortunately, the terrain was flat, and only one vehicle passed them coming the other way, its headlights illuminating the crystallizing snowflakes. Soon a neon sign came into view and the truck slid into the drive. Lew jumped out and retrieved the tire from the back of the truck as a middle-aged mechanic greeted them. His greasy blue overalls smelled of gasoline, he chewed on something, and wiped his hands on a shop towel as he walked up. A yellow curl fell over one eye.

"Well, how can we help you? Looks like Charlene's old Ford! You relatives of hers?"

"No, just customers. We ended up with a flat tire in front of her shop."

"No spare?"

"Used the spare back in Fresno," Lew answered. "We weren't expecting another flat. Charlene lent us her truck to get here. So, can you fix our tire or not?"

The man laughed and called to someone inside the garage. "Hey Ray, folks are here with your ex's jalopy." Spitting on the ground, the man took the tire from Lew. "Yeah I can fix it. It'll be $45."

"Kind of a high price for fixing a flat, wouldn't you say?" Dallas argued.

"Next stop is twenty miles down the road, but I don't think that rattletrap of Charlene's will make it that far. It's got a rod knock. Besides, everything'd be closed by the time you got there."

Dallas pulled out his wallet and counted the cash. Before he had time to offer it, the man snatched it out of his hands and rolled the tire into the garage. Lew and Dallas followed.

There was an oil barrel stove putting out heat inside. A radio made background noise, the static scratching the atmosphere. A man sat leisurely in front of the stove nursing a cup of something that smelled like alcohol. Too many pimples for his age, he had a sizable nose, unwashed hair, and brilliant blue eyes. He chewed on the tip of an empty pipe while he sized Dallas up. After regarding Lew the same way, he took the pipe out of his mouth.

"Which one of you two courtin' my ex?" Ray asked.

Dallas' cheeks burned.

"Neither of us. We just borrowed her truck to find somewhere to get our flat fixed," Lew said.

"Right."

"Soon as we're done, we'll take the truck back to her and head on to the ski lodge."

Dallas frowned. Why should they defend themselves to this man?

Ray laughed. "No, you won't. Road's closed."

"We've got chains," Dallas said.

"Closed," the mechanic interrupted as he threw the tire on the spreader and applied soapy water to find the leak. "Can't travel up the mountain, not even with chains. They've got three feet of snow already."

Dallas looked at Lew. His friend had his hands in his pockets. Steamy breath leaked out of Lew's mouth when he sighed.

"Is there a motel in town?" Dallas asked.

"Nope, not anymore. Folks who owned it moved away this fall." Ray said. "Looks like you boys will be spending time in the back seat of your car. Or that truck," he laughed. "Maybe Char baby has an extra rug on the floor for ya." He stood up, stretched, and walked into the shop.

Once a plug had been put into the tire, the mechanic bounced it on the ground in front of Lew.

"Have a good evening," he said.

Dallas was glad to leave. He liked neither of those men. Unfortunately, Charlene's truck had stalled while they were in the garage. Lew pushed from the rear, and Dallas at the driver's side until they had the vehicle rolling. Dallas hopped in and popped the clutch, Lew jumped in and they crept slowly toward town.

Flashing yellow lights at the junction they'd need to take to the mountain verified the mechanic's story. The highway to the lodge was barricaded with a Road Closed sign.

"I guess that does it," Lew said. "They weren't lying, at least."

"With Charlene's generosity, I was beginning to think this was a friendly town," Dallas said.

"You think she set us up?"

"No. But I think she had a serious problem with that man. Probably still does. I can see why she divorced him."

"Yep." Lew agreed. "He's a loser all right."

They were silent for a few moments, Dallas peeling through his thoughts.

"What does Christmas mean to you, Lew?"

"Christmas?" Lew sat silently for a moment. "I was never religious. I grew up with five brothers and a sister so there wasn't much in the way of presents although I got my first bike at Christmas when I was seven. You know L.A., though. No seasons there so it was mostly about good food, parties, and plenty of alcohol when we got older. Girls liked to shop but not me. Why?"

Dallas shrugged. "Just thinking about Charlene handing me the keys to her truck. She didn't have to be so generous. Our problems weren't hers; you know."

"True."

"Our family celebrated Christmas a little differently. My parents taught my sister and I that the holiday wasn't just about receiving things. We'd volunteer with a local non-profit by helping the blind, took them shopping so they could buy gifts for their loved ones."

"You grew up religious?"

"Not religious, but with an appreciation for God and Jesus."

Lew huffed and looked out the window. "Fairy tales."

"Call it what you will, Lew. I like to help those who need help. That's what Jesus taught. Nothing make-believe about it. We should be kind. Treat people well."

"Not everyone deserves to be treated well," Lew mumbled and wiped the steam off his window.

"Granted, it's not easy a lot of times. I wasn't sure where that Ray fellow was coming from," Dallas agreed.

"Jealousy. Apparently, the man hasn't let go."

When they got to the shop, Dallas turned up Oarlock Street and made it halfway up the hill. When he stepped on the clutch to change gears, they rolled backwards. Dallas engaged the tranny and hit the gas. Tires spun; the truck skidded sideways. Lew held onto his seat and laughed.

"Park on Main Street," he said when the Ford finally stopped rolling backward. "I doubt Charlene's going anywhere. When she does, from the looks of it, we'll be here to help push."

They parked behind the Jeep in front of the shop and Dallas cut the engine.

"Once we get that tire on, then what?" Dallas asked.

"We could get something to eat at that diner."

Snow still fell, covering their coats, their wool caps, their noses, and their eyelashes. In a way, Dallas was glad not to return to the lodge. True, a warm bed awaited him there, but he'd already become invested in this town. He had met a lonely woman, her ex, and an ungrateful investor. The dark side of a quaint little community with all the charm of a Kinkade painting.

"I wonder if our ski jackets wouldn't be of some help for Meritville," he said.

"Who in this poverty stricken town could afford a solar powered jacket that lights up by a phosphorescent membrane?"

"No one," Dallas answered. But hadn't

41

they made enough money with the crowdfunding campaign to gift one or two? He didn't say anything. They had come with boxes of the jackets, which were stacked up in the back of the Jeep, adults', and children's alike.

The cold found its way under Dallas's scarf by the time they finished putting the tire back on the Jeep, and even though he'd put on warm socks that morning, he could barely feel his toes. Clouds darkened to a haunting blue as the day moved into twilight. Lew locked the Jeep and Dallas went into the shop to return the keys. Charlene stood by the cash register talking to an elderly woman, so he waited by the door.

"I'm just devastated," the woman said.

"I wish I could help you, Mrs. Jameston. I have very few Christmas items in the store. Nothing for teenagers, really."

"Yes, I know. I'm just venting. It's just that those poor children have been through so much, what with the fire and all."

"I understand perfectly. I have no home."

"I know you've had enough trouble of your own." Mrs. Jameston patted her hand. "I know."

"I still have some piggy banks."

Mrs. Jameston laughed. "My grandchildren already have Meritville piggy banks. Filled with pennies too. I don't know a single soul in town that hasn't purchased one of your banks. Or your candles." She looked over her shoulder at Dallas. "I'd better get back to the house. Looks like you have a customer."

Dallas held the door open for the woman. She nodded a thank you.

"Such a gentleman!" she said. "My husband always held the door open for me. Such a nice feeling." She patted Dallas on the hand, nodded and left the shop.

Dallas brought the keys to Charlene.

"Your truck wouldn't make it up the hill. I'm sorry. But if you need to go somewhere, it looks like Lew and I will be around to give you a push."

Charlene took the keys and stuck them in her pocket.

"I can try to park it on Oarlock Street again if you want."

"No, you're fine."

"Thank you, again, Charlene." He knew she was unhappy—with him, perhaps, with the truck not being parked as she had asked, or perhaps because she couldn't come up with something for Mrs. Jameston's grandchildren for Christmas.

"Is there something I can do? To help out?"

"Do you perform miracles?" Charlene asked.

Dallas shook his head.

"Then, no."

The Diner

"Christmas is hard on a lot of folks this year,"
-Jill

*E*very door in town must have a bell attached to it, Dallas thought, for when Lew stepped inside the diner, a jingle drew the attention of the three customers, the waitress and the cook. Dallas nodded and followed Lew to a table. A fireplace lit the back corner of the building where a Christmas tree glittered with baubles. Stockings hung over the hearth. A pile of firewood rested in a cast iron log holder. Candles wrapped in evergreen boughs flickered on the tables. The scent of Christmas blended with savory aromas from the kitchen.

"Make yourselves at home," the waitress said with a grin and brought them each a menu and a glass of water. "The name's Jill. Travelers, I take it?"

"Yes, Jill," Dallas answered.

"Let me guess, you got stuck in Meritville because the roads are closed?"

Dallas' cheeks flushed.

Lew laughed. "Yes, it appears that we did."

"Well that's unfortunate for you, and fortunate for Meritville, I'd say."

Her smile was contagious.

"Soup today is corn chowder, vegetable, or beef stew. We have chili too. Take your time, we don't close until nine." She strutted away to clear a table across the room.

Dallas opened the menu, a simple list of breakfast foods, burgers, and two full dinners, spaghetti, or meatloaf. The smell of comfort food caught his attention. He glanced at the fire and found himself mesmerized by the contentment it gave. Meritville might be poor, but it had a flavor of home, one that he had longed for all his life. He didn't get this sense of well-being in Los Angeles.

"I think I'll have the meatloaf," Lew said. "I wonder if they have beer here."

"Beer?" Dallas asked. "Kind of cold for beer."

"Gin and tonic, then."

"I don't see any alcohol as an option, Lew. You might have to settle for something milder. Like a soda, or tea."

"Tea?" Lew closed his menu and took a long swig of water. "There's probably a bar in this town. No sane person lives in a town without a saloon."

"We need to figure out where we're going to sleep before we go on a binge." Dallas studied the menu, not sure what to order.

"If we spend the night drinking, we won't

need a place to sleep," Lew reasoned.

"Even bars close at night, Lew." His friend wasn't serious. If anyone towed the line, it was Lew. He just liked to talk as if he were a sot, but Lew had higher morals than most anyone Dallas had come in contact with. If he didn't have integrity, Dallas wouldn't have asked him to be a partner on his project.

Dallas was the fashion designer; Lew was the scientist that made their project unique. They spent last year perfecting their jacket, and this year they ran a huge campaign that brought in hundreds of thousands of dollars, giving them a marketing advantage. Ski lodges and other prestigious corporations were now purchasing their line and begging for the science behind it. Lew was shrewd, though, and kept the patent a secret. What the two of them were doing on this trip, besides taking a vacation, was introducing their jacket to skiers and anyone who might enjoy an ultra-warm, streamlined wrap that lit up at a touch. An Awareness Trip, Lew called it.

"Then you tell me. Where are we going to sleep?" Lew took another drink of water. "Comfortably, that is. Because if you suggest the Jeep, I'll roll you across the street and make a snowman out of you."

They had paid a heavy price for two rooms at the lodge, and now they had no way to get there. Granted, the reservation was good until after the first of the year and they had already enjoyed a few days of skiing. Meritville had simply been a day trip to satisfy their curiosity, be it an untimely one.

"I suppose we're just going to have to trust that something will come along," Dallas suggested. He could try the spaghetti, but he wasn't that fond of tomato sauce.

"Trust?" Lew shook his head and snickered. "Trust what? Your god?"

Dallas shrugged. "Yes."

Jill returned to take their order.

"Well, boys, what have you decided?"

"I'll take the meatloaf, and—," Lew flipped the menu over. "A coffee, and a room."

Jill wrote the order down on her receipt book with a smile and turned to Dallas.

"Same," Dallas said.

"You want the room over-easy or scrambled?" she teased.

"Sunny side up," Dallas laughed.

"Okay," she said and picked up their menus. "Coming right at ya."

"See?" Dallas said.

Lew gave him the finger.

The meatloaf came steaming hot with a pile of mashed potatoes and gravy, green beans on the side and a fruit bowl. Jill returned to pour their coffee and Lew frowned.

"The room?" Lew asked, his hands spread

wide, palms up.

"It's still in the oven," she said and winked at Dallas.

Dallas had not tasted a better meal in a long time. What Meritville didn't have in prosperity, it had in cookery. Both he and Lew forgot about conversing, they were so involved in the meatloaf and potatoes. Once they devoured most of their food, Dallas slowed down.

"I need to not eat too fast," Dallas said, coming up for air.

"Impossible," Lew argued, sipping his coffee. "I could almost forget that we're homeless, this food is so good."

"Let's not remind ourselves," Dallas snickered.

Before they finished eating, Jill returned with their tab and set it on the table.

"Here's the deal. If the temperatures are what they say they're going to be, you can't sleep in your vehicle. Meritville doesn't want anyone to freeze to death because the mortician's out of town."

Lew nodded. "Seems reasonable."

"So, one of you can drive me home. I walked to work this morning not knowing we were in for a blizzard. It came a day early. I have a spare room. It's not big enough for two people, though, and one of my nephews is on the couch. So, I arranged for the other of you to stay the night with one of my friends. I already talked to her so you're cool. She lives across the street in the Cozy Home Gift Shop."

"A spare room with a bed?" Lew asked, anxious. They both knew the gift shop had no such accommodations.

"You go ahead, Lew. I can sleep on the floor." Dallas said. That, and he'd like to see Charlene again.

"Charlene has a sheepskin she'll lay out. She used to raise them—sheep, that is—before her ranch burned to the ground. Poor girl is really feeling things right now. So just let her know you're grateful and don't pry. Her life is bad enough what with her ex banging on her window every night. The fella's a real loser. Spends more time in the drunk tank than he does out of it. I think a little righteous company for her will put her mind at ease. Christmas is hard on a lot of folks this year after this summer's forest fire."

"There was a fire?" Lew asked.

She set the coffee pot down after pouring them another cup.

"Almost three hundred thousand acres of our mountains were burned. Most of it was national forest, but some of it was private property. Hundreds of homes and ranches in the area. Three people died, two of them firefighters. A lot of people just up and moved away. Charlene's parents did, but she wouldn't let them sell the shop. She has this crazy idea that she's going to make enough money selling to tourists to rebuild her home. Maybe get her horses back." Jill shook her head. "She's my best friend. I think she's nuts for trying, but she won't hear it. All I can do is encourage her."

"She's a strong woman," Dallas commented. "I admire her tenacity."

Jill raised her eyebrows. "She told me you two were by, trying to sell some sort of project to Mr. Atwater."

"It was a foolish mistake. We tried to apologize."

"Bah!" Jill waved her hand. "Getting a rise out of that old coot was probably a good thing. Got his heart pumping for a change. Charlene felt bad after you left, said she'd acted foolishly. She probably won't apologize. She keeps her defenses up, but she'll treat you right."

Lew gave Dallas an odd look, one that Dallas couldn't figure out.

"I have to close the diner tonight. If no one comes in by eight, I'll shut her down early. Can you stay that long?" Jill asked Lew.

"I'm not going anywhere." He crossed his arms and leaned back with a smug smile.

"You'd best head over to the shop when you're finished eating, Dallas. Charlene doesn't stay up late."

"You know my name?"

Jill grinned. "Charlene told me."

Dallas laughed. Small town!

He folded his napkin, stood, and tossed a bill on the table. "Keep the change, Jill. And thanks for your help. Thanks for putting my friend up for the night, too. Keep him in line."

She winked. "Will do."

An Icy Storm

"The stranger did not lodge in the street: but I
opened my doors to the traveler."
- Job 32:32

*C*harlene wasn't accustomed to visitors,
especially not overnight and certainly not
male. Why did she let Jill talk her into this?

She stumbled down the stairs with an
armload of blankets, the sheepskin balancing
on the top. After the wildfire ravaged the town,
gifts from Lewisville came. Plenty of blankets,
and even a couple of quilts were offered. They
had been distributed to everyone who lost their
homes. Charlene had been given a fair share.
Certainly, she had enough for an overnight
guest. Who was she to withhold generosity when
others had been so generous to her?

She tossed the bundle on the floor where
she had moved the tables, wondering if he'd
rather sleep nearer to the fire. She shrugged. He
could decide.

She didn't begrudge offering hospitality
to Dallas. It's just that, well, he was a man,
and she had sworn not to have anything to do
with men. Her ex had been the reason for that.

53

Sill, she felt bad for the way she had acted that morning.

They hadn't stolen any business from her. Mr. Atwater's daily dollar-fifty could hardly be classified as supportive to her shop. She snickered and shook her head. An apology was probably in order.

Imagine, crying in front of a complete stranger!

She knelt next to the stove and layered firewood over the embers. The vent squeaked when she turned it and the flame blazed. She shut the door to the stove. So hot did the fire flare that the stove pipe glowed red where it met the potbelly. Charlene adjusted the flue, taming the roar inside the cast iron. Lured to the warmth that emitted from the hob, she stood near the stove pipe and absorbed the heat.

Enough wood had been stacked in the log holder to last until morning. Perhaps Dallas would bring some in when the firewood ran out. It'd be nice to have a man help her with some of the chores, even if it were for only one morning. She'd been accustomed to doing everything herself and sometimes it wore on her.

No, she thought. That's absurd. She couldn't ask this stranger to work. He was, after all, a guest. She chuckled to herself. *Dallas? Already on first name terms? Not a good sign.* Perhaps she should call him Mr. O'Neill. That would be much more appropriate.

Charlene spread the blankets out over the sheepskin, piling them up until they made a soft bed. Pleased with the aesthetics, her job was done. She put one of the dining chairs by the fire and sat down with her book.

She could not get herself to read, though. Wind blew wickedly outside. The sign above her shop door banged viciously against the wall, creaking, and groaning like that of a haunted house. If not for the Christmas lights, the night would have had the eerie quality of a Halloween celebration.

With no warning, the power went out, leaving only the glow of the stove pipe and a little bit of light that radiated through the cracks of the potbelly's door.

"Shoot. There it goes," Charlene complained.

A bell jingled and a knock told her Dallas had arrived. She sighed, relieved that she didn't have to spend the stormy night alone. Setting her book down, she brushed her hair back over her shoulders, and straightened her powder blue sweater.

Dallas stood on the other side of the door; his image seen through the glass. Huddled and shivering, he waited patiently with a pack on his back while Charlene stumbled through the dark to let him in.

"It's a nightmare out here," he said as he stomped the snow off his boots on the floor mat. "A charming town just lost its charm! I can't tell you how grateful I am for your hospitality. I don't know what I'd do if I had to sleep in our vehicle."

"Take off that wet coat and hat and come warm yourself by the fire."

She had to lead the way through the dark. Rolling her hand over a shelf where she kept an emergency stash of matches. She found the candles she was supposed to be selling and unwrapped one and lit the wick. The candlelight gave Dallas' face a soft radiance. His hazel eyes caught the spark of the flame. Yes, that was an Irish nose—upturned a bit—his hair matted and wet from the snow. The smile he gave her sent a tickle up her spine. He *was* good looking!

"You must be freezing," Charlene said.

"Warmth immediately enveloped me as soon as I stepped inside, both from the temperature of the room and from your hospitality," he said.

Charlene raised her brow. Such verbiage. A gentleman. She was not aware that such creatures even existed anymore.

"I've brought some blankets down for you. I wasn't sure if you wanted to sleep in the dining room or over here by the fire."

"By the fire, most assuredly. I'll even keep

it stoked for you so that this place stays warm all night. It's cold out there."

He set his pack down and took off his coat, holding it by the stove to dry. His turtleneck sweater revealed a healthy torso, a man who either worked or worked out. Or both, perhaps.

"I have hangers if you want to hang your coat on the wall behind the stove. It should dry by morning."

Charlene hurried up the stairs in the dark to her room and rummaged through a box on the floor where she kept her hangers. She had no closet. The room she slept in was only meant to be a storage room for the shop. She paused, her heart racing from the jog up the stairs. Why was she making such an effort to please this man? Hadn't she learned her lesson? She used to cater to Ray, running to fulfill his every whim. What did it get her? Too often a fight. A black eye sometimes. Tears. A broken home. Shame. She took a breath and calmed herself.

Using the handrail of the stairwell to find her footing down, she returned to the shop and handed Dallas the hanger. He had a flashlight in his hand. A small little battery-operated knickknack he was using to see inside his backpack. He nodded a thank you, put the flashlight in his mouth and took the hanger, stretched his coat over it and hung the garment on a nail behind the stove.

"Want to see something cool?" he asked.

He held the pen-sized flashlight against the coat. At first Charlene thought the glow was made from his flashlight but when he moved it, a red and green line followed, as if the light had been a paintbrush and the coat a canvas. The florescent pigments stayed. He continued to move his hand in swirls and circles until the coat shone with multicolored shapes. When he took his hands away, the coat glowed in the dark room with a collage of patterns and colors.

Charlene gawked.

"This is our project. We've been working on this for two years and finally raised enough of a fan base and financial support that some of the major clothing chains are picking it up. I designed the coat. You won't find another style as efficient against winter weather as this one. It also can fold up to a compact size for backpacking. It could even save your life on the slopes if you get lost. Lew did the chemistry."

"That's amazing! Simply beautiful."

"Thank you." He turned to her, beaming.

"How long will it stay lit?" She asked.

"Quite a while. If you don't want it to shine anymore, you give it a good shake down. Want to try it?"

He handed her the flashlight. Not knowing what to write, Charlene drew the only thing she knew how to draw. A heart. She stepped back and realized she had left her scribble on the jacket sleeve.

"Very telling," he whispered.

Telling indeed! How could I have done something like that? Charlene thought as her cheeks flushed. Time to retreat!

"You must be tired, and I need to open the shop in the morning," she said and nodded toward his bed. "Do you need anything? There's water in the kitchen if you get thirsty. The restroom is down the hall beyond the kitchen."

"Thank you," Dallas said and put his backpack on the chair.

"Good night."

"Good night. Sleep well," Dallas answered.

She ran back up the stairs, locked her door, changed into her nightgown, and collapsed on her bed. Leaving that situation was the best thing she could do. Why had she complicated her life by being so transparent to a stranger? Of all things, drawing a heart on the sleeve of his jacket. What a fool! She wanted to cry but he might hear her and that would be just as revealing.

If only life was the way it used to be. Hunkered down on stormy nights at the ranch with her folks had been safe, cozy even. Their old dog, Germaine, knew the difference between the wind and a bear, or a cougar. He'd bark at the one and growl at the latter. Germaine died two months before the fire. She missed the big mutt, but he had lived a long life.

With family around, Ray never drove out to the ranch to harass her. Not until she moved into town had he begun his stalking. He was the biggest mistake she ever made, and because of that she guarded herself from ever having a relationship again, even though she wanted one. She wanted to love someone, and to feel loved, but it was just too risky.

If you can't work together with someone toward a common goal, you might just as well work alone.

That had been her motto ever since her divorce. She wondered if marriages were indeed a dying tradition, something that faded away with her parents' generation. God knows, she didn't want one ever again.

She glanced out the window. The clouds had lifted enough that she could see them floating by, the silver of the moon casting a portentous glow. The snow had ceased to fall, and now the cold swept over Meritville. What didn't topple from the wind or the weight of snow, would crack and fall simply from brittleness. Was that what was happening to her? Were the storms in her life making her stiff and breakable? Was she doomed to ruin because there was no flexibility in her heart?

Didn't Christmas mean anything to her

anymore? Was kindness simply a cover up? Or could she once again dive into her soul and find the Christ that once kept her alive and loving? It was beyond her power to change. She'd been too wounded.

A tear leaked from her eye and trickled down her cheek.

"Please let me love again," she whispered before she fell asleep.

Charlene woke to a loud noise coming from downstairs. Not sure if it had been a dream, she sat up and listened. Again, there was a bang and a rattle. Charlene jumped from the bed and grabbed her robe, her heart thumping. *Not again, not tonight!*

The noise continued.

The fire burned in the pot belly stove, and Dallas was up, fully dressed, staring at the door with a look of confusion. Charlene couldn't see past the shelving in the store, but she could guess what the commotion was. It's happened before.

"It's Ray," she growled. "My ex."

"What does he want?" Dallas asked.

"Who knows. He's probably drunk. He does this often. He'll freeze to death out there though if I don't let him in."

"You're going to open the door?"

"I have to." Charlene lit the candle and found her way through the shop. Once at the door, Ray swore, his voice louder than the wind. Always a filthy mouth, she wished he'd go away permanently. Charlene put the candle down and unlocked the entry. As soon as the door cracked open, Ray pushed his way in, shoving Charlene backward. She would have fallen but for the arms that caught her from behind.

Once Charlene got her balance, Dallas flew in front of Charlene and caught Ray's fist. Ray lunged forward and Dallas braced himself, resisting the man's body weight. Ray fell into him. Dallas grabbed both of Ray's arms and drove the drunken intruder back out the door.

Ray spat in Dallas' face. Dallas looked over his shoulder at Charlene, a wad of spittle dripping down his forehead.

"Is there a sheriff in this town?" He asked, struggling to keep Ray from squirming loose.

"Yes."

"Call him!"

Ray cursed again. He tried kneeing Dallas, but Dallas dodged away still holding Ray's arms. Ray panted and drooled; his scowl fixed on Charlene.

"Don't you call the cops on me, woman!"

Her heart pounding, Charlene reached for her phone by the till and dialed Sheriff Bandon. He lived not far from her, walking distance even. When the sheriff answered sleepily, she caught her breath,

"It's Charlene. Ray's here drunk, throwing his fists around."

"I'll be right there," the sheriff said. "How are you protecting yourself?"

"I have a guest helping me," she answered. Dallas glanced at her.

Ray lost his energy and sunk to the floor with Dallas still holding onto him. Nonsensical filth poured from his mouth. He looked up at Charlene after she slipped her phone in her pocket.

"You called, didn't you? You're nothing but a..."

"Shut up," Dallas interrupted. "Leave her alone. She has enough trouble without you adding to it."

"Good!" Ray responded. "She deserves everything she's getting." Ray spat on the floor next to him. Soon he lowered his head, mumbling, closed his eyes and to Charlene's relief, began snoring.

Dallas released Ray and stepped away. Charlene retrieved the box of tissues and wiped Dallas' face, lingering long enough to lock eyes with him.

"Thank you," she whispered.

"That fist was meant for you. How could he?" He choked on his words, still breathing hard, his face still red with anger.

Sheriff Bandon came in his SUV and

Dallas helped take Ray to the car. The sheriff locked the door and followed Dallas back inside.

"I'll give you a call in the morning to file the charges. Breaking and entering?"

"No, I let him in."

The Sheriff rolled his eyes. "Charlene, I've told you before not to let him in. He means nothing but harm to you."

"What was I to do? Let him freeze to death?"

"Just call me. If you let him inside, we can only keep him locked up long enough for him to sober up. Right now, he's going to be sleeping in a cell but at least it will be a warm cell. Just warning you though, he'll be out in the morning."

"I let him in because I don't want him breaking my windows. I can't afford it."

The sheriff nodded and then shook his head.

"Power's out at the jail house. Not much more can go wrong tonight. Who's this fellow?" he asked, nodding at Dallas.

"Dallas O'Neill," Dallas answered. "My friend and I came for the day from the ski lodge and were waylaid by a storm."

Sheriff Bandon tipped his hat. "Thank you for watching over Charlene."

The sheriff turned back to her before he walked out the door.

"Merry Christmas."

Charlene snickered. "Right. Merry Christmas."

The shop was a dismal dark when she and Dallas turned to the fire. He knelt, opened the stove and stoked the fire.

"The man is dangerous," Dallas said, his eyes fixed on the flames.

The fire cackled as sparks rose from the embers. "It's a shame that relationships have to end this way. It's a shame they have to end at all, but this..." He shook his head.

"I'm sorry to involve you. You really didn't need to see my garbage." She held her hands up to the fire and absorbed the warmth. He stood across from her, on the other side of the stove. The coat of color on the wall still glowed, the heart she had drawn still glimmered on the sleeve.

"You didn't involve me. And that garbage isn't yours. You gave me a place out of the cold for the night and your ex just happened to show up. I think he would have hit you if I hadn't intervened. Stopping him was a natural thing for any man to do. That wasn't your fault."

She conceded. She'd had enough counseling after the divorce to know not to blame herself for Ray's actions.

"Still—"

"How long were you married?"

"Three years. I honestly didn't know he had a drinking problem until six months into the marriage."

"I see. That makes it hard to trust anyone now, doesn't it?"

Charlene caught his eyes and nodded.

"And yet you trusted enough to take me in for the night, so all is not lost." He smiled.

"No. I suppose there's still hope for me."

"Are you a Believer?"

Charlene nodded.

"Good." He stared again at the fire.

Is Dallas an angel?

Charlene asked herself as she lingered near him. Tonight he looked like one, the red of the firelight made his skin glow.

Charlene remembered she was still in her bathrobe. Not very appropriate clothing to wear around strangers, nor around the sheriff!

"Excuse me. Morning will come before we realize. I need sleep."

"Of course," he said. "Rest well."

Christmas is coming

"The world is full of magic things, patiently waiting for our senses to grow sharper."
-W.B. Yeats

Morning had indeed come before Dallas realized, and this morning was Christmas Eve. Something magical had to happen today. Something good had to show itself. He stretched his arms and rubbed his matted hair. Sleeping in his clothes had not been comfortable and tackling a drunk in the middle of the night hadn't helped either. He threw the covers aside and wandered through the empty store to peek out the window. Snow no longer fell, but clouds still hovered low. Icicles dripped from the awning over the shop. He had tried to keep the fire going but had fallen asleep. The room was chilly and smelled of burnt wood and cold ash. Looking at his watch, he knew Charlene would be up soon to open shop.

He rolled the blankets and the sheepskin into a bundle and set it behind the counter. Pulling the tables back where they belonged, he placed the chairs around them. In the kitchen,

67

Dallas looked for a pot and filled it with water and, being as the electricity was still down, he set it on top of the potbelly stove. One lone piece of firewood remained in the log holder. Smoke puffed out at him when he opened the door to place the log on top of the coals. A turn of the flue drew the smoke up the chimney and blowing on the embers started a flame.

The colors had faded from his jacket, but still dotted across the bodice. With one shake, the streams of light faded away. He put his jacket on and without a word, Dallas slipped on his gloves and went outside, holding the bell on the door so that it didn't ring and wake Charlene.

Surprisingly, the streets were filled with children. Two boys and a girl sped down the hill in a sled kitty-corner from where he stood. Directly across the way, in front of a boarded up storefront that, according to the sign used to be a cobbler's shop, youngsters put their finishing touches on a snow fort, and other boys and girls on his side of the street were in the process of constructing their own. A rosy-cheeked young man skidded into him when Dallas stepped outside.

"Whoa, there!" Dallas exclaimed as the boy grabbed Dallas' coat to keep from slipping on the icy sidewalk. Dallas caught him and helped him gain his balance just as a snowball plodded into Dallas' back.

"What's your name?" Dallas asked.

"Jimmy," the boy said, panting, his freckled face glowing from the cold morning air. "Our fort's not done and already they started attacking."

"We don't need a fort. Let's give them what for. Come on, I'll help you." Dallas said and waved to the boy's companions as he scooped a mound of snow off of the hood of Charlene's truck. He formed a snowball, packed it tight, and handed it to Jimmy, gathering more snow for himself.

"Charge!"

Guiding the boy away from Charlene's truck and her vulnerable storefront window, he stepped into the street. Jimmy and his friends joined Dallas, and together they threw their projectiles at the fort. Dallas' snowball split on the fort wall and spattered snow in the faces of three rivals. Jimmy ran away and Dallas, laughing, scurried up Oarlock Street, a volley of snowballs hitting his backside. Icy wet crept under his collar. He shivered, wiggling his shirt to free the snow from under his clothes.

"Hey! Come back," one of the rivals yelled out to him. Dallas shook his head and laughed.

"Later!" he promised.

He had remembered seeing a pile of firewood in the alley behind Charlene's building the day before, so he hiked up the hill well out of range of any snowballs, unless the boys decided to ambush him. The wood pile had diminished to a handful of logs, so he assumed it was a community resource.

Loading what was left, he brought the firewood back down the hill, only to be met with a barrage of cold wet snow in his face. He shook his head, licked the snow from his lips, and hurried to the shop. Opening the door with two fingers so as not to lose his load, he quickly entered with a ball of snow splattering at his feet. He shut the door, unable to hold in his laugh. Snow spewed over the floor from his coat, his hair, and his pile of logs.

Charlene looked up, startled. She wore a holiday sweater and had braided her hair. She looked beautiful. The shop was toasty warm.

"They're merciless!" he laughed.

"Those rascals!" she scowled.

"Merry Christmas!" Dallas greeted, stomping the snow off his boots. "Sorry about all this wet!"

"That's not your fault," she answered.

"Oh, I'm afraid it is. I got them good earlier."

"Did you?"

"I'd forgotten how much fun it is to play. Sorry about tracking snow into your shop."

"You've got to stop apologizing. You saved me the trouble. Thanks for getting the coffee water started. And moving the tables and..." she looked around the shop. "...And everything. I overslept. Mr. Atwater will be here for his coffee soon."

"Mm, there's something to look forward to. Perhaps I should leave."

"Don't be ridiculous," she answered.

"By the way, the firewood pile in the alley is nearly diminished. I'm willing to cut more if I knew where to go."

"I've been hauling logs from my ranch. I have a huge pile of rounds that my father and his friends cut for me before they left for Europe. He figured no matter where I lived, I'd need wood and the property was the best place to store it. It just needs to be split."

"You've been hauling all the wood? What if I make a trip out there today?"

"You'd get lost by yourself. I'll ask Jill if she'll watch the shop today and we could both..." she paused as their eyes met. "...I mean, we could both go. I guess."

"I would like that, Charlene," he said, not surprised at her reluctance. For what she told him last night, and what she'd been through recently, he was surprised she'd go anywhere with him alone. Perhaps today he could gain her trust.

The kettle on the stove whistled just as Mr. Atwater walked in the door with a newspaper.

He stopped short and gave Dallas a cold glare. Dallas smiled and nodded at him.

"Merry Christmas," Dallas greeted.

Mr. Atwater walked over to his favorite table and tossed the paper down.

"Coffee done?"

"Almost, Mr. Atwater." Charlene poured the hot water into her French press and coffee aroma filled the shop.

"Tree fell down in my driveway. Electric's out. Nothing merry about this Christmas. Keep your religion to yourself," he told Dallas.

Dallas raised an eyebrow and shared a glance with Charlene.

"Need someone to get that tree out of your driveway?" Dallas offered.

"Already got it covered," the man said.

Charlene poured Mr. Atwater his coffee and offered a cup to Dallas. Dallas took his and strolled to the window, figuring he'd leave Scrooge alone.

He eyed Charlene on her phone, hoping she was texting Jill. Mr. Atwater was a pill to be around. Dallas would rather spend the day alone with Charlene. A little hard labor would do his body good, since he couldn't ski. He watched her from his spot by the window.

He had much more than sympathy for her. The more he talked to her, the more he enjoyed her company. Perhaps the challenge of breaking through her wall of mistrust challenged him. Or perhaps her transparency enticed him, a vulnerable and yet powerful woman. She was also incredibly good looking, her eyes alluring.

"I suppose you want an apology for yesterday," Mr. Atwater mumbled. "Well you're not going to get one. And if you think you're going to apologize to me, I won't accept it. I know your kind. You see someone reading the financial section of the news and right away you think you're going to get something out of them."

Dallas looked around the store and placed his hand over his heart.

"Are you talking to me?"

"Darn right I'm talking to you. Who else would I be talking to?"

Dallas strolled over to his table.

"It was a misunderstanding," Dallas reasoned. "But if you feel that I should apologize, then I'm sincerely sorry."

Mr. Atwater set his paper down. "Misunderstanding? Bogus. I know exactly what you were doing."

"If you don't want an apology, then what do you want?"

"I want to see you and that long-legged friend of yours out of Meritville."

"Mr. Atwater, come now," Charlene interrupted and walked to the table with her hands on her hips. "Dallas meant no harm to you. There's no reason to even bring yesterday's misunderstanding up again unless you mean to cause trouble. It's Christmas Eve. I don't want trouble today."

"Oh! I see! We're using first names with the stranger now, are we? This tidbit joker rides into town one day, the next morning he's in your shop like he owns the place."

"That's unfair," Charlene argued.

"Unfair? I've been your customer for over a year, Charlene Donne. I come in here and buy a newspaper and a coffee from you every day. Who else does that here in Meritville? I know your family like I know the back of my hand. I used to talk with your father for long hours. Even ate your mother's cooking. So now here I am, your steady customer and you're going to defend this transient over me?"

Charlene rolled her eyes.

"Mr. Atwater, I'm not defending anyone. I'm simply asking you to let it go. Let's be at peace today."

'Peace!" Mr. Atwater huffed. "That's how you feel? Peace?" He stared at Charlene and she glared back.

Dallas waited for his cue to jump in, but it seemed she had control of the situation. The man snorted, stood, his face flushed red, and his gaze switched back and forth between Charlene and Dallas.

"Very well. I'll let you have your peace!"

He stormed toward the door, took one look back at them, and left.

"He had a bad night." Dallas offered as an excuse for the man.

"I hope I never get that old and cranky," Charlene grumbled. "If ever there was a Bah Humbug, that's him." She turned quickly to Dallas and pointed her finger at him. "And don't you apologize."

"Yes, ma'am," Dallas said, hiding his smile behind his cup. The coffee tasted good this morning. Maybe because of the French press, or maybe because of the server. "You handled that confrontation quite nicely, by the way,'" he added.

"You think?"

"I admire a woman who stands up for herself. Don't mind one who stands up for me, either. Thank you. You're remarkable."

Charlene blushed.

"Jill will be here in a few moments. With Lew," she said.

The Ranch

"Where there is love there is life."
- Mahatma Gandhi

*A*s much as I complain about this old beater, it always seems to get me where I need to go," Charlene explained as she, Lew, and Dallas pushed the truck down the snowy road. "And if it doesn't start, or if it stalls, all it needs is a little encouragement."

"And a lot of elbow grease," Lew added, panting.

With it coasting downhill, she and Lew stopped pushing. Dallas, at the driver's side, jumped in the cab and got the engine started.

"Thanks, Lew," Charlene laughed and ran to the vehicle as Dallas backed it up.

"Have a good time," Lew encouraged.

She would. Charlene swore she wouldn't let the pain of her past get in the way of whatever the day would bring. The sun had peeked out from behind the clouds this morning, and even though the power still hadn't lit up the town, people were on the streets enjoying the snow.

"It's nice being a passenger for a change," Charlene said.

"I'm glad you think so. I enjoy driving. I

had to ride shotgun all the way from L.A."

"Lew did all the driving?"

"He's possessive with his Jeep. Rightly so. It's a nice ride. Keeps us moving."

"So, you travel a lot?"

"Just this year. We're working on getting the word out about the coat of many colors," he laughed.

"That wouldn't have been a biblical reference, would it?" Charlene smiled. She enjoyed his sensitivity. The observation about the heart on the sleeve last night had been perceptive. Almost poetic even if it did embarrass her.

"The meaning is up to the observer," he answered. When he looked at her, the twinkle in his eye gave her chills. "I don't like to push my faith on other people, but I won't deny it either."

"I'm the same way," she agreed, then leaned forward and pointed. "You'll need to take Barringer Road. Up here to the left. There's no sign, you just have to look for these two special trees."

"I'm a city boy, Charlene. The trees all look the same to me." Dallas laughed. "Will I need four-wheel drive?"

"Probably not. The snowplows keep these back roads cleared. The two men who drive them live out this way."

"I like that about Meritville. It's so personal!"

"Right here!" Charlene pointed and held onto her seat as the truck bounced over the mound of snow that the plow had piled up on the drive. The truck wheels skidded but caught traction as soon as Dallas straightened the wheel.

"How far up the road?" he asked, spinning the steering wheel, and skidding around an icy puddle.

"Not too far. Once you see the remnants of a burned forest, you'll know we're there. Ours was one of the last ranches to get hit."

Weathering the bumps and pitches of the snowy lane, passing the neighbor homes that had survived the fire, Charlene pointed to a hill and tracks that had been filled over with last night's snowfall.

"That's it," she said. "Just go as far as you can. The wood pile is to the side of what used to be a house."

Dallas turned the truck around and backed up the hill until they started skidding. He parked and shut off the engine. Charlene jumped out and waited for him. She was used to coming here. The devastation didn't affect her anymore, but she could tell the ruin affected Dallas by the way he stood there staring at the lone brick fireplace. Her smile faded when their eyes met.

"This was your home?"

"It was a beautiful house. Two stories. A farmhouse built in the thirties."

He walked slowly to the old fireplace and touched the bricks, regarding the chimney.

"It must have warmed the upstairs too."

"The chimney ran through my bedroom. I was always nice and toasty in the winter."

"A great loss. An estate, no doubt. I'm sorry."

Charlene shrugged and turned away from him in case she started crying. The wound of loss was still fresh.

"What's done is done. If you can't go back, you have to go forward," she said. "The property's still mine. I could rebuild, someday. If I ever get the money." That last sounded hopeless. She wasn't going to earn enough money with her shop in Meritville, and she knew it. Jill knew it. Dallas could make the same assumption. What would probably happen is that she would have to sell the property to afford a place to rent. Hopefully, her discouragement didn't show. She didn't want to live in despair. She wanted to believe in a miracle.

"Let's get your firewood." He gave her a warm smile and held out his hand. She paused for a moment, not sure if she should accept, but before he drew his outstretched arm away, she reached out.

"Anything is possible, you know," he said quietly as he took her hand in his and squeezed it. "Stay strong."

They walked hand in hand to the woodpile. Just being near him kept her warm. How often had she come up here by herself? How long had she been living a lonely life defending the walls she'd been building around herself? Walls that wanted to shut people out. Walls that prevented her from trusting anyone.

"Load me up," Dallas said and knelt near the pile of wood.

She placed firewood into his arms until the stack reached his chin.

"More," he encouraged.

"I'll bury you in wood," she laughed.

"It's okay. I can handle it."

She stacked another few pieces of wood on top. He hurried through the snow to the truck and dumped the wood in the bed, pulled down the tailgate and jumped in. By the time she brought her load to the truck, he had stacked his pile neatly up against the cab.

As she assumed would happen, the clouds darkened the sky soon after they arrived at the ranch, and before they had the pickup filled, snowflakes began to fall.

"Do other people in town pull from your pile?" Dallas asked.

"They do. And other people also add to the pile."

"Then let's keep loading until the snow starts getting heavy."

She was fine with that, glad that he had suggested it. She enjoyed working with Dallas. Right now, the assistance that Dallas was giving her instilled her faith in men. She didn't want to admit it, but the more she watched him work, the more attractive he was. Kind, thoughtful, soft spoken. Well read. Intelligent. He was the sort of person she needed to be around. She hadn't ever been around a man who made her feel creditable the way he did.

Like Jill, he seemed to be the kind of friend who stuck by your side even when your chips were down. Dallas came into Meritville to tell the world about a beautiful jacket he designed and instead, here he was hauling firewood, pushing a deadbeat truck, and changing flat tires in the icy cold, with no complaints.

By noon, the snow seemed to be as thick in the sky as it was on the ground.

"We'd better go," he suggested when he finished stacking the load.

When they returned to town, Dallas backed the truck up Oarlock Street and parked by the alley, so unloading wasn't near as difficult as loading had been. Once they had the logs out of the truck, he picked up the axe and started splitting.

"You don't need to do that now," Charlene said. "Come inside and get warm. We've been in this snow half the day!"

"I wanted to demonstrate to you what a good coat this is," he laughed.

She gave him a frown.

"I'll split enough wood for tonight. Go on inside and I'll bring some wood in when I come."

"I'll make cocoa," Charlene offered.

"I'm looking forward to it!" Dallas said.

She grabbed an armload of wood and hurried down the hill, careful not to slide. When Charlene walked into the shop with her arms loaded, Jill, Lew, and Mrs. Jameston were seated at one of the tables.

"Merry Christmas, Mrs. Jameston."

There was no answer, but Charlene was too excited to notice. The trip out to the ranch, the fresh frosty air, and the budding relationship with Dallas invigorated her. She dumped the wood on the floor and stacked it neatly in the log holder on top of what Dallas had brought in that morning.

"I see the power's still out."

"Charlene," Jill said.

"It's okay though, we've got lots of wood, and candles, and we'll do something for Christmas. Maybe some kind of potluck or something. I'm not sure what but I can feel it in my bones that it will be a happy one." Charlene smiled at the three. They had not returned her enthusiasm.

"Charlene," Jill repeated. "Mrs. Jameston's house is freezing cold.

"We brought back a truckload of wood, Jill. There's plenty, Mrs. Jameston."

Charlene noticed Mrs. Jameston's red eyes. The older woman held a handkerchief over her mouth.

"Oh, I'm sorry, Mrs. Jameston." She rose and pulled up a chair, scooting it close to the elderly woman. "We'll get your house cozy warm, don't worry."

"Lew and I will go," Jill said. "We were already planning on it."

"That's not the only problem," Mrs. Jameston said. She wiped her eyes and glanced at the door when Dallas walked in.

"My grandchildren are here. They had a rough journey what with the snow and all. My daughter and her husband almost turned around and went home the roads were so bad, but fortunately they were able to follow the snowplow in. I feel like such a horrible grandmother." She dried her eyes and folded her hankie.

"Nonsense. Mrs. Jameston. You're a terrific grandma."

"I have nothing for the children in the

way of presents. My daughter and her husband are not well off. They've always looked to my husband and I to help with Christmas. I know it's silly to feel this way, but they're special children and I want to give something to them."

Charlene knew Mrs. Jameston's grandchildren and she had nothing that a teenager would be interested in. Candles, and soaps, and knickknacks that would be boring for teenagers. She wished she'd been able to stock her shelves this summer with all that had been on her wish list, but everything fell apart when the town had been evacuated. Nothing had been the same since.

"How old are your children, Mrs. Jameston?" Dallas asked.

"Twelve and fifteen. A boy and a girl."

"Christmas isn't just about gifts, you know," Jill said

"I know. And they already gave me plenty of hugs and told me they were okay with not having any presents, but...well, I guess it's just me. I just want to see my grandchildren happy."

"Happiness isn't in things," Jill said softly. "It's the love that's important. You give plenty of that."

Mrs. Jameston cleared her throat and stood. "I need to be getting back. The house is really cold, and my husband is frail, you know."

"We'll load up my SUV," Jill said. "There's

plenty of room for a load of wood. Lew can drive us up the hill to get it." She grinned. No one with any sense enjoyed driving up Oarlock Street in the snow, even if the wood pile was so near.

"Why don't you all stop by here tomorrow morning," Dallas said. His offer silenced everyone in the room. "Bring your grandchildren. Jill, bring your nephews. What other children are in this town? Bring them. We'll...we'll celebrate together."

Charlene cleared her throat after the lull.

"That sounds like a wonderful idea. I have spiced apples we can have for breakfast. Perhaps we can put up some more decorations. Sing some songs."

"Let's do it," Jill said.

The Eve of Christmas

"Oh, I know that there's hope for me in the afterlife! The thing is, I'll be on the far side of heaven away from everyone else." - Charlene

*C*louds had settled over the town again, and the short daylight hours were swiftly fading away. It was dinner time, but without power, Charlene couldn't cook unless they heated something on top of the potbelly stove. Without electricity, the diner wouldn't be open.

"Do you like green beans?" Charlene asked. "I have some jars of green beans I canned this summer. I'll bring one down and we can heat them up. You must be famished."

"Good idea," he agreed and carried another chair over by the stove. It was cozier that way, Charlene thought.

They ate quietly together. She had such a grand time this afternoon with him that now she felt awkward not being able to fix him a decent meal. Here they were, two strangers basically, eating a measly dinner of green beans that had been grown in her garden only months ago. She set her fork down, her stomach upset.

"This is too bizarre," she said.

He glanced up at her.

"The beans are delicious. Just the right amount of salt and pepper and butter to taste. You needn't feel embarrassed about this dinner. It's food, isn't it? I'm grateful."

"I wasn't exactly embarrassed about the food," she said.

"Something else is bothering you?" He set his fork.

"Well, yes."

Was it right to tell him? She didn't know him, really. She was attracted to him, but what did that mean? That she was still a young woman with some life left in her. What did it matter if she wore her heart on her sleeve?

"I wish I knew you," she started. "I wish I had already spent more time with you so that we had established a friendship. You're a gentleman and a joy to be around but..." Oh, good heavens, was she really going to say this? She choked on her words. "...But I know you will be gone tomorrow."

When he frowned, she corrected herself. "Maybe not tomorrow, but the next day, or whenever it is that you and Lew are leaving. And then you'll be just another memory. Like the ranch. Like my horses, or my old dog, or all the other lovely things that had come into my life and are gone now."

Why was she telling him these things?

She had no control over these words. They were pouring out of her mouth like a fountain, and there were more.

"And I'll be left alone to struggle through each day, a penny at a time."

Charlene shook her head, knowing she should stop but she had no self-control. She had to talk to someone. There was too much bottled up inside.

"My savings will dwindle. Meritville will no longer be on the map if we continue to have fires every year. People will leave. More shops will close. I'll never be able to rebuild my ranch. I don't think the pieces will ever be picked up again. How can they be? I have this shop now, but for how long? I can't live upstairs, I'll be evicted come spring and the shop isn't providing enough profit for me to rent a place. Then what? Then I'll have to sell the ranch."

Here come the tears.

"I'm not feeling sorry for myself. I'm just saying it like it is. All that was beautiful is now gone. Everything. Even my self-respect. Oh, I know that there's hope for me in the afterlife! The thing is, I'll be on the far side of heaven away from everyone else. The lower forty. Maybe where the old cows are put out to pasture! Excuse me."

She rushed to the counter where her till was, where she kept her tissues. She blew her nose and turned her back to him. Dallas stood when she got up.

The poor man, she thought. *What did he do to deserve this?*

"I'm sorry," she said and shook her head.

Don't!" he replied so sharply that she spun around.

"Don't apologize," he said. "You've lost so much." His voice quieted, his words almost inaudible if the room hadn't been so still, she might not have heard him. "Such a compilation of tragedy for one person to bear. I have not had half the misfortune in my entire lifetime that you have borne in a matter of months. I think if it were me, I would be wallowing in my bed refusing to open my eyes to daylight. And yet look at you. You've done all of this and helped others along the way. Please. Don't apologize for anything."

His words were delivered so tenderly that Charlene burst into tears. She hadn't seen him approach her. How could she, blubbering like she was? His strong arms were around her and when she opened her eyes, she was leaning against his chest. He brushed her hair with his hands and held her. His arms were healing. He let her cry.

She hadn't ever released so much stored emotion in her life. She felt drained. She reached for a tissue and moved away from Dallas. Bowing her head, she took the box with her and sat by the stove. Dallas followed.

"I'm done wallowing," she said, forcing a laugh. "It's Christmas Eve. Good things are supposed to happen tonight. Santa Claus and all of that. Usually in the past Meritville was filled with the spirit of Christmas. Look what's happened. An entire community down in the dumps." She wiped her eyes dry and tried to laugh. A sorry attempt at sounding cheerful, she gave up. "You have something planned for tomorrow it seemed?'

"I do. Or shall I say we do. Lew and me. But first tell me how many children, would you say, live here in town?"

"At the moment, maybe twenty if that many. Some of them are teenagers. There are a few toddlers. A lot of our residents go south for the holidays, even more this year because of the fire. You invited the entire township to the shop?"

"They won't all have to come inside. We can meet them in the street." He shrugged. "Though it is cold out there."

"I don't mind. We can move things around. It's a small shop but I doubt everyone will be coming all at once. Tell me your plan."

"I'll show you."

With that, Dallas went outside to Lew's Jeep and came back a little later with several large boxes stacked in his arms.

"There's more where this came from."

Lights

"This is how he was taught to celebrate Christmas—by pleasing others and offering hope to those who were hopeless."

*C*arolers could be heard down the street, and as Dallas strung the rope through the sleeves of the last jacket and tied it up to a hanger on the wall, he ducked under the row of garments and looked outside.

"They're coming our way," he said. He jumped from the shelf. "I think Meritville is about to have a Christmas Eve party, Charlene."

The warmth in her smile sent a chill through him. This is the sort of Christmas his parents had taught to celebrate, to please others, and offer hope to those who were hopeless.

Why had he become so involved in such a short time with not just an entire town, but with this one special woman. He watched her as she pulled the paper cups from out of the cupboard and lifted the lid of the large kettle on the pot belly stove. The aroma of spiced cider so sweet, and Charlene so beautiful.

The shop was alight with color glimmering against a dark background. Charlene's silhouette radiated the blues and reds and greens, and to see her full of life gave Dallas satisfaction. She deserved so much more than the hand she'd been dealt.

When Dallas stepped outside all he could see in the storefront window were hearts and stars and the holiday greeting of *Merry Christmas*. The jackets illuminated the snowy scene below them. A Christmas tree, statuettes of skaters on a pond made from a mirror, bundles of presents gift wrapped with bows iced with glitter. Even the frost that had collected on the storefront window outside and the icicles on the awning reflected the festive colors that had been written on the jackets. He and Charlene both wore their own works of art. Their little corner of the world couldn't have been more magical!

The carolers were a group of young people organized by a local scout troop. They were accompanied by Santa Claus aboard the local vintage fire engine.

"They carol every year rain, snow, or cold. I always give them cider, but this year is going to be different, isn't it?" she asked. "This is exciting."

If nothing else, seeing Charlene smile made being stranded in Meritville worthwhile. She had such beautiful dimples. But there was more besides his affection for her. The whole town would be blessed tonight!

The engine's horn sounded as the carolers

made their way across the street to the shop. Dallas stood by the door, his arms crossed, his jacket covered with drawings of shooting stars and holly leaves. Charlene had chosen to cover hers with hearts.

Squeals of delight rang out when the carolers neared. The Cozy Home Gift Shop was the only business lit up with more than candles and lanterns. Mrs. Jameston's grandchildren were with the singers, as were Jill's nephews. Curious neighbors who hadn't been a part of the caroling group strolled over the snowy road toward them. The children were so excited to see the display that they had to be reminded what they came for. Soon the song "Deck the Halls," resonated throughout the streets.

With rosy cheeks and noses peeking out from wool hats and holiday scarves, the children harmonized with such heavenly voices that the melody seemed to echo off the stars. They sang a collection of carols and ended with "Silent Night."

The charm of Meritville had returned. Dallas' heart swelled with joy, and tears moistened his eyes. This tight community had worked so hard to survive. Tragedy had taken its course here but despite the heartache these people experienced, Meritville was showing its vigor tonight. He was pleased to be a part of the restoration. When Charlene, smiling and laughing with the children, came and stood by him and locked her arm into his, he took her hand and held it tight. When had he ever felt so much a part of something? Never!

Like Charlene had tried to express earlier, he too didn't want this moment to end. He glanced at Charlene, her voice ringing in song with the carolers.

"'Tis the season to be jolly!"

What could be more beautiful than this sort of joy?

By the time they opened the door and let everyone in, it seemed that the whole of Meritville had come for the celebration. Mrs. Jameston's grandchildren let out a loud "whoa!" when Dallas handed them each a jacket and showed them how to color them.

"Oh dear!" Mrs. Jameston held onto Charlene's arm; tears of joy welled in her eyes.

Charlene gave her hand a squeeze and brought Mrs. Jameston a box of tissue.

Jill's nephews were thrilled with their jackets which they covered with symbols and faces for dragons.

"Gaming lingo and logos," Jill explained as she sipped cider with Dallas and Lew.

"The coats fit perfectly," Lew observed.

"This is the warmest coat I've ever had," Jill said.

"We should probably give the rest of these away while everyone is here," Dallas suggested.

"Sounds like a plan," Lew agreed.

Lew and Dallas unstrung the coats, matching sizes to the carolers and visitors. Even the parents and the troop masters received a jacket, and there were still more in the Jeep. Dallas and Lew showed the children how to create the patterns and demonstrated how to erase the markings and start over. The gathering could not have been a happier Christmas Eve party. Soon the teenagers were outside flashing through the streets, their arms streaking color as they tossed snowballs and played tag.

"No one has to worry about whether they are having a good Christmas," Charlene said, tucking her arm through his.

He pulled her closer to him.

Not Goodbye

"If I had a flower for every time I thought of you...I could walk through my garden forever." -Alfred Tennyson

*C*harlene woke to a bright room and the central heat puffing into action. Relieved that the power had returned, she turned off the lamp, fell back down on her pillow, and gazed out the window. High clouds floated through blue skies, reflecting the golds and pink of sunrise. A clear day!

It's Christmas.

She smiled, reminiscing on the events of Christmas Eve and how thrilled the children were. She also recollected the warmth and love from Dallas and her smile faded.

She didn't want to lose him, but she would.

We've only known each other for what? Four days? He lives in L.A. He's a big-time entrepreneur. He might even be famous someday soon with his name in all the fashion magazines. He'll probably marry some gorgeous model with

99

high cheekbones, silky hair, and an hourglass shape. Someone with as much money as he has, why wouldn't he?

The bell to the front door jingled. Charlene looked at her watch that lay on the floor next to her bed. *Good heavens, it's almost nine o'clock.* She threw the covers off and scurried to dress, fix her hair, and celebrate the holiday with a touch of mascara and blush. She hadn't showered for how many days now? It was horrible, living like this. Jill would let her shower at her house later, after everyone went home and the town returned to normal. After Dallas and Lew left.

She pouted and drew in a breath.

When she descended the stairs, Mr. Atwater was at the table, and Dallas had made the man's coffee for him in the coffee maker. Surprisingly, they were talking quietly to each other. What sort of Christmas miracle was this?

"Merry Christmas, Mr. Atwater," Charlene greeted. "And Dallas,"

"Good morning," Dallas returned.

"I see you two are talking," she whispered to Dallas.

Mr. Atwater stood, a pout on his face.

"I saw the shenanigans going on in here last night," he said. "I wasn't sure your father would have approved. He's an even-tempered man with common sense and a fair intellect about financial matters."

100

Charlene raised her brow. "My father gave me this shop. It's mine free and clear. If I choose to give out apple cider on Christmas Eve, I shall do so, with or without your approval."

"Cider is not my concern," he grumbled.

"Then what is your concern?"

"Throwing about one of the best lines of ski jackets anyone will probably ever see. Do you know what those coats are worth? And you gave them away to the entire town."

She eyed Dallas, who stood against the wall, his arms crossed, his head bowed.

"Why are you worried about coats that don't belong to you, Mr. Atwater?"

"Because I just made a deal with this fine young man. I now have stock in those coats. I aim to make you an offer as well."

That's why Dallas' head is bowed?

"What kind of deal?" Not so sure she wanted to do any negotiating with Mr. Atwater, she crossed her arms and waited, keeping her eyes on Dallas as well.

"If I'm going to be a share holder in this project, I would like to have a place where these coats can be distributed exclusively. That won't be completely possible as Mr. O'Neill here has already signed some contracts with other distributors, but if your shop carried these coats with an exclusive label signed by O'Neill and his partner, we'd have a monopoly on that market."

101

Finally, Dallas looked at her, a pleasant smile on his face.

"How is that going to work, Mr. Atwater? I can barely stay afloat as it is, and I'm not going to sell my ranch to keep the shop. I want a place to live, and I can't live here."

"Let me invest in your shop," Mr. Atwater said. It was more a demand than a plea, but that was how the old coot was. "I'll write you a check today. I've seen the excitement on the recipients of these coats last night. They are the best thing that has ever happened to Meritville. Can you imagine the tourism from the ski lodge alone when we open with product?"

"You want to invest in my shop?"

"What do you need to stay in business? 500k?"

Charlene's mouth dropped and she gawked at Dallas. He shrugged.

"We'll discuss profits once we negotiate a retail price. I know a good investment when I see one. I'm not much of a philanthropist, never saw the profit in giving things away, but having a hometown with a stable economic future protects my own investments. Well? What do you say?" He pulled out his billfold.

"I guess," Charlene answered, still stunned.

"You guess?" Mr. Atwater shook his head and took out a check, sat at the table and wrote it out.

"I have a lawyer who will help write out a contract. This is for you today. You'll get the rest when we sign."

He handed her a check and offered a handshake.

A little sudden, Charlene hadn't much time to think about selling a share of her store, but what else was she going to do? If Mr. Atwater is an investor, he would take care of the finances and perhaps all these projections concerning the jackets would come to fruition.

"I have to live here until I can find somewhere else to live."

"You have forty acres," Mr. Atwater argued.

"With no house."

He nodded to the check. "Get yourself an RV. We'll be making enough money to build your house. This is big time, Charlene. Your father would do it. Do you know how many ski lodges there are in the United States? Do you know how many fashion magazines are already pumping this project?"

Charlene took the check and Mr. Atwater picked up a package off the table. Evidently Dallas had given him a jacket. With a thumbs up, he walked out the door. "See you next week, after the first of the year when the bank is open."

Charlene was frozen. How could it be?

103

"Merry Christmas, Charlene," Dallas said.

"You did that?" she asked.

"He came up with it on his own."

"How?" she fell on the chair and stared at the check he had handed her. "It's not just money."

"No. It's not. But money helps. You *will* be able to rebuild. You'll have your ranch back."

He smiled and sat across the table from her.

"And you?"

Dallas shrugged again; his eyes lowered. "I have commitments."

"Of course, you do. You're in the thick of this."

"I've fallen in love with Meritville," he whispered. "I've...well, I've fallen in love with you."

The sunlight caught the color in his eyes. Her heart raced. Was he really saying that? Or was she in a dream having yet to wake?

"I have commitments right now that I have to fulfill. And I know that you've spent your life trusting people and they've failed you. I don't know how to leave and promise you I'll come back and have you believe me. I will, but I don't know how I can convince you."

Charlene swallowed. What could she say? She stood when he did. She wanted to be closer to him in this moment. Her insides trembled.

104

"Yesterday," he started, his words slow and thoughtful. "When I held you, I knew I needed to be with you. You fulfill something inside of me that I didn't know I needed until I came here. A purpose. Something more than just creating a jacket that will sell."

He offered his arms and she stepped into his embrace. He kissed her hair.

"I'm a pretty cautious person. I take time to make decisions, weigh the pros and cons. This is indeed quick for me. I've been here only four days, but you have been on my mind the entirety of those days, and nights I might add. That's not to say I've given myself enough time to make a resolution. I promise you, though, I will not decide otherwise without returning to you." He stepped back and took her hands. "I think we could make a life together, if you'd have me."

The blood rushed out of her head. Her heart raced. Her knees turned to rubber and if he hadn't been holding her hands, she might have fallen.

"I... I hope you'll return quickly," was all she could mutter.

"Of course. Lew and I are headed to the lodge as soon as the road clears. I'd like to take you skiing. If you can close the shop for a few days."

She laughed. With what Mr. Atwater gave her, she could close the shop for a month. But she wouldn't do that. After her divorce, she had sworn that she wouldn't lose herself completely over another man. No. She would stay focused. Get strong. Heal. And then if she and Dallas did have a future together, she'd have something to offer the relationship.

"I would like that," she said.

"After the first of the year I have to fly back to L.A. and close some deals, sign some contracts. I'd like to find a place to rent here in Meritville. Give us the time we need to get to know each other better."

Charlene nodded. She couldn't peel her eyes from his. He sighed and smiled at her.

"You're beautiful, Charlene. Not just pretty, but your heart, your strength. I'm so glad Lew and I were snowed out of the ski lodge for Christmas. It seems it was meant to be."

He tucked her hair behind her ears, his touch so light, so tender. He stroked her cheek gently and then their lips met. She lost herself in his kiss.

The End.

Acknowledgements

I want to thank my good friends Kim Mutch Emerson and Gwen Whiting for their support, encouragement, and critiques as well as helping to edit the manuscript. I want to thank Lorri Moulton for her encouragment also. It's amazing how much we depend on each other through our writing processes. As always I thank my husband for supporting me and putting up with my attitudes when I'm frustrated.

I was thrilled to write this novella. It was a lot of fun and though it's still technically the end of summer, I can feel Christmas coming on. It doesn't help that the power went out the same time it went out in Meritville!

Have a very happy holiday season and if you enjoyed this book, please leave a review.

I'm D.L. Gardner - Author, screenwriter, story teller. I write fiction for young and young at heart folks who like a tall tale and a fast moving adventure. I've written ever since I was a youngster and have led an unusual life after that, having grown up in the sixties, lived in the desert for nearly 30 years in a mud hut, raised horses, sheep, goats, chickens, and seven children.

Much of my life experience has morphed into my stories. Storytelling is my passion. I believe a story should endure time and be good enough to hand down from one generation to the next.

To see more of my work, please visit my website https://gardnersart.com

Ian's Realm Saga books 1-3
    Layla Born at Night 3.1
    Fallen Morning 3.2(currently in draft state)
    Diary of a Conjurer 4
    Cassandra's Castle 5
Thread of a Spider
An Unconventional Mr. Peadlebody
Altered
Where the Yellow Violets Grow
Dylan
Novellas and short stories
Lost on Taikus
Sasha
Tale of the Four Wizards
The Far Side of Heaven

www.ingramcontent.com/pod-product-compliance
Lightning Source LLC
Chambersburg PA
CBHW050804250626
47155CB00005B/2205